COUNTDOWN
TO THE YEAR 1000

For John Kleuser
—K.H. McM.

Dragon Slayers' Academy™ 8

COUNTDOWN
TO THE YEAR 1000

By K.H. McMullan
Illustrated by Bill Basso

GROSSET & DUNLAP • NEW YORK

Library of Congress Cataloging-in-Publication data is available.

McMullan, Kate.
    Countdown to the year 1000 / by K.H. McMullan ; illustrated by Bill Basso.
    p. cm. — (Dragon Slayers' Academy ; 8)
    Summary : Alarmed by a prophecy that the world will end with the arrival of the year 1000, the students of Dragon Slayers' Academy get some advice from Zack, a boy who has traveled back from 1999.
    [1. Prophecies—Fiction. 2. Millennium—Fiction. 3. End of the world—Fiction. 4. Dragons—Fiction. 5. Schools—Fiction. 6. Time travel—Fiction.] I. Basso, Bill, ill. II. Title.
    PZ7.M47879 Co 1999
[Fic]—dc21   99-054541

ISBN 0-448-42033-3 (pbk)   B C D E F G H I J
ISBN 0-448-42054-6 (GB)   A B C D E F G H I J

Chapter 1

"ray, what is this?" Wiglaf asked. He gazed at a bowl of dark, slimy mush as he inched forward in the Dragon Slayers' Academy cafeteria line.

Angus sniffed at the stuff. "Smells like eel," he said.

"It must be seaweed," Erica put in. "There are no more eels to be had for free from the castle moat. And Headmaster Mordred would never pay for eel."

"True," Angus agreed. "But my nose says it's eel. Uncle Mordred must have figured out a cheap way to get some." Angus was the headmaster's nephew. He knew all about his uncle's penny-pinching ways.

"Hold your plates out, lads!" called Frypot, the DSA cook. He dolloped some glop onto Wiglaf's plate. "Here's my new dish. I call it Millennium Surprise."

"Yes, but what is it?" asked Angus. He was plump and quite fond of a good supper.

"Just eat it," Frypot replied. "Next!"

Erica, Angus, and Wiglaf carried their trays to the Class I table and sat down. Torblad and Baldrick were already there, shoveling the mysterious meal into their mouths.

"What is this supper?" Angus asked them.

"Eel," Torblad said in his gloomy voice.

"I knew it smelled like eel!" Angus cried. "Where did Uncle Mordred get it?"

"From the moat," Baldrick replied. He wiped his ever-runny nose on the back of his hand. "'Tis a new type of eel. It costs next to nothing. And it can live in the filthiest water."

Wiglaf never thought he would wish for a bowl of his mother's cabbage soup. It smelled awful and tasted worse—especially toward the end of the month. But now he remembered it fondly.

Wiglaf had left his home in Pinwick with his pet pig Daisy at his side. He had come to Dragon Slayers' Academy to learn to be a hero. He was redheaded, freckle faced, and small for his age, so he did not look much like a dragon slayer. Yet Wiglaf had—by accident—killed two dragons already.

"Doom is upon us!" a voice boomed out suddenly. "The world is coming to an end!"

A hush fell over the dining hall.

Mordred jumped to his feet. "Who said that?" he cried.

"The duck, Uncle." Angus pointed.

Indeed, a large white duck was waddling toward Mordred on wide orange webbed feet.

"Doom! Doom!" cried the duck. "In two days' time, the world will end!"

"Oh, what does a duck know?" said Mordred. "Begone from here, fowl quacker!"

"But, sir!" said the duck. "It is I, your scout!"

"Yorick?" cried Mordred. "Back from Toenail so soon?"

Yorick yanked off his duck head and nodded. "And with dire news!"

He pulled a piece of parchment from a pocket of his duck suit. He waved it in the air. "This prophecy of doom is nailed to every tree in the Dark Forest!" he said. "Listen!"

And Yorick began to read:

"The year 1000 fast approaches,
None will survive except the roaches.
Say hello to Armageddon,
For that is where we're surely headin'—
Earthquakes, firestorms, flaming pits,
Black plague, brown plague, gas pains, zits."

Wiglaf listened with growing alarm. Could this prophecy be true? Tomorrow would be the second-to-last day of 999. There was talk about a year 1000. But what sort of year had *four* numbers? It was a very scary time.

Yorick kept reading:

> *"How to know the world will end?*
> *Beware these signs, my frightened friend:*
> *When chickens bark and dogs me-ow,*
> *When pig-faced calf is born to cow,*
> *When fish are kept in golden cages,*
> *Then bid farewell to Middle Ages!"*

Everyone in the DSA dining hall gasped. Wiglaf pulled his lucky rag from his pocket. If ever he needed luck, it was now.

"Alas and alack!" Mordred cried. His gold rings clicked together as he wrung his hands. "Yorick, go back out to the Dark Forest. Gather more news. And this time, make it *good* news!"

Yorick thrust the prophecy into Mordred's hands. Then he turned and waddled out of the dining hall.

"The end of the world," Mordred muttered. "Oh, woe is me!"

"Woe is all of us, Uncle," Angus said.

Wiglaf turned to Erica. He knew that she was smart. She fooled Mordred by dressing as a boy so she could go to all-boys DSA. She was really Princess Erica, daughter of Queen Barb and King Ken. Only Wiglaf knew her secret. Now he wondered if Erica was smart enough to know whether there was any truth to this dreadful prophecy.

"Psst!" Wiglaf said to get her attention. "Do you believe what Yorick is saying?"

Erica shrugged. "Perhaps *The Sir Lancelot Fan Club Handbook* has some advice for us," she said. She pulled the dog-eared book off her tool belt. She began flipping the pages.

Wiglaf sighed. If the world was going to end in two days, he did not think even Sir Lancelot could stop it.

Chapter 2

"tab it!" Mordred told Wiglaf the next afternoon in Slaying Class. When Coach Plungett left on his honeymoon, the headmaster had been too cheap to hire a new teacher. So he took over Slaying Class himself. "Just do it, boy!"

Wiglaf took a step toward Old Blodgett, the practice dragon. But he could not bear to stab even a cloth-covered dragon stuffed with straw.

CLANK! CLANK!

Wiglaf eagerly turned to see what was clanking. A knight stood by the gatehouse. He was covered from head to toe in gold armor.

"Hear ye! Hear ye!" the gold knight cried.

He banged the shaft of his golden spear on the ground. "I bring word from Count Upsohigh, the Count of Castle Cashalot."

Erica leaned toward Wiglaf. "I know this castle," she whispered. "It is made of gold stone and stands on a hill above the town of Toenail."

"What of it?" Mordred cried. "What has Count Upsie-daisy to do with me?"

"Count Upsohigh can stop the prophecy from coming true," the gold knight replied. "He has a clever plan."

"What, pray tell, is that?" said Mordred.

"He shall make," said the knight, "a Golden Hippopotamus!"

Mordred raised one bushy black eyebrow. "A golden one, you say?"

"Solid gold," the knight answered. "Everyone in the kingdom must bring all the gold they can find to Castle Cashalot before midnight tomorrow. Count Upsohigh must have one hundred druckets of it, or his plan shall not work."

"One hundred druckets!" Wiglaf gasped.

"Why, that is a thousand struckets!"

"It is ten thousand gluckets!" Angus added.

Erica grabbed the ink pot, quill, and scratch pad from her tool belt. She scribbled furiously.

"Sir knight!" she cried at last. "That is one hundred thousand bluck-bluckets. Surely there is not so much gold in all the world!"

"You must hope that there is," the knight replied. "For unless Count Upsohigh has exactly one hundred druckets, the plan will fail. And then the world shall come to a terrible, horrible, unbelievably bad end."

"Tell us his plan, sir knight!" Mordred cried.

"Count Upsohigh shall melt one hundred druckets of gold in a giant cauldron," the knight explained. "He shall pour it into a mold of a huge hippopotamus. Then, at the stroke of midnight on the last day of 999—"

"Doom!" cried Yorick, bursting suddenly into the castle yard. His orange duck feet flapped as he ran. His feathers were a mess.

"I met a peasant in the Dark Forest!" Yorick

cried. "He knows of a farmer in East Armpittsia whose chickens are barking like dogs!"

"What?" cried Mordred.

"Chickens, sir!" Yorick said. "Instead of *cluck, cluck* they say *bow-wow*. Or maybe *arf-arf*. Could be *woof-woof*! I heard them not myself, sir. But word in the Dark Forest has it that the chickens made a noise exactly like that of a dog."

"What of it?" Mordred sounded annoyed.

"The prophecy, Uncle!" Angus cried. "Remember? It said, 'When chickens bark'!"

"Good King Ken's britches!" Mordred cried. "So it did."

"See? There is not a moment to lose," the gold knight warned. "Gather up all the gold you can find. Bring the gold to Castle Cashalot by midnight tomorrow. Or the world shall surely end!" The gold knight bowed. "Now I must be off to warn the folks at Dragon Stabbers' Prep."

Mordred's violet eyes followed the knight as he hurried out of the gatehouse. Then he turned to his students.

"Go to your dorm rooms, lads!" Mordred cried. "Get dressed for dragon hunting. Report back to the castle yard in..." He checked the hourglass he wore on his wrist. "...ten minutes. You shall go to every dragon cave in the Dark Forest. Grab what gold you can and bring it back here, on the double. And don't go getting burned to a crisp by the dragons," he added. "Not at a time like this. Go on, now. Go!"

The students ran for the castle.

"Hold it, Angus," Mordred added. "You and your friends, come here."

"Yes, Uncle." Angus hurried over to Mordred. Wiglaf and Erica ran after him.

The headmaster glared down at the three.

"I want you to go up to that room at the top of the South Tower," Mordred said. "The one with the books."

"You mean the library, Uncle," Angus said.

"Whatever," Mordred said. He handed Angus the parchment with the awful prophecy. "Show this to Brother Dave. Ask him to give you every single map of dragon caves in the Dark Forest. And none of his guff about not ripping pages out of books."

"Yes, Uncle," Angus said. He rolled up the prophecy and stuck it inside his tunic.

"And hurry up about it!" Mordred called after them. "We haven't a moment to lose!"

The three ran up the South Tower staircase. Huffing and puffing, they burst into the library.

The DSA librarian looked up from his book as they came in.

"Good day, good students!" Brother Dave exclaimed. "Art thou here to check out books? I have some dandy new ones that thou mightst enjoy. *Running from a Dragon*, by Willie Makeit. 'Tis a most exciting tale. So is *The Dark Night*, by Kent C. Innything."

"Sorry, Brother Dave," Angus said. "But we are here because Mordred wants maps of dragon caves."

Brother Dave sighed. "Waitest thou here. The map file is down in the dungeon storeroom. 'Tis not easy to get to. It may take me some time." So saying, Brother Dave went off.

"While we wait," Erica said, "let us look up hippopotamus."

Wiglaf walked over to a bookshelf. He pulled out Volume H of *The Encyclopedia of the Middle Ages*.

"Hip...hippo," he muttered as he turned the pages. "Here it is."

They looked down at a drawing of a large beast. It had a rounded head and four sturdy legs. Wiglaf tried to imagine a solid-gold hippo.

Suddenly, they heard a commotion outside. Wiglaf put the book down. They all hurried over to the slit in the castle wall and peered out.

Yorick was running toward the castle, yelling, "A butcher in East Ratswhiskers told a candle maker in Toenail that a dog in Pinwick was heard me-owing like a cat!" Yorick cried. "The prophecy is unfolding! Doom is upon us all!"

Pinwick? Wiglaf thought. Why, he had grown up in Pinwick. His mother and father and twelve brothers lived there still. Had they heard the dog me-ow? He felt a small pang. He missed his big, messy, nasty-smelling family.

Wiglaf sighed. He left Angus and Erica at the window and went back to the encyclopedia. When he picked it up, he frowned. How odd... The words on the page seemed to have stretched. Were his eyes playing tricks on him? He blinked. But that only made things worse. Now the page seemed to bulge up out of the book. Wiglaf dropped the book in fear. He stepped back. The page kept swelling bigger and bigger. It looked as if something was *inside* the book! Something that was trying to get out!

"Egad!" Wiglaf cried.

Erica and Angus ran over to him.

All three stared at the strange shape rising from the book. Then came a horrid ripping sound.

The page split open.

Out fell what looked like...a boy.

Chapter 3

gad!" Wiglaf cried again.

He stared down at what surely was a boy. But he looked like no boy on earth. He wore a strange multicolored tunic. His leggings were blue—unheard of! And on his feet he wore... There were no words to describe his unsightly black-and-white boots.

"Zounds!" cried Erica.

"Yoiks!" Angus added. "Where did *he* come from?"

"He grew out of this book," Wiglaf said. "But we need fear him not, for he is dead."

At that moment the boy's eyes opened.

"He is alive!" cried Erica.

All three jumped back.

Wiglaf stared at the boylike creature. His thoughts whirled.

And then the creature uttered strange sounds.

"Uh, hi," he said. "What's up?"

"He is talking!" cried Wiglaf.

"But he speaks not in English," Erica said.

"That is because it is not a real person," Angus said. "It is a demon! It popped right out of that book. What else but a demon could pop out of a book?"

The demon sat up. It stared at them. Wiglaf trembled. At any moment, flames might shoot from his evil-looking eyes.

"What did you think it said?" Angus whispered to Wiglaf.

"Nothing," Wiglaf answered. "Just sounds."

"It *wasn't* just sounds," the demon said.

Wiglaf jumped back again.

"It was words," the demon insisted. "And it is so English."

Wiglaf felt frozen to the spot. The demon had quickly picked up their tongue! What other awful tricks might it do?

Erica drew her sword. She stepped forward. Wiglaf wondered where she found her courage. Did she not know that demons could slay humans with a look?

Erica pointed her sword at the demon.

"Pray, sir, who are you?" she asked. "A demon?"

"No," the demon answered. "A boy. Just like you."

"He is a demon!" Angus cried. "Demons speak in tongues. Demons speak whatever language you do. And they pretend to be just like you!"

"Where *am* I?" the demon asked.

Wiglaf was sure this was a trick question.

But Erica answered, "You are in the library, sir."

"The one on Forty-second Street?" asked the demon. "It doesn't look at all familiar."

Wiglaf frowned. The demon spoke English. But he was hard to understand. What was this forty-second street he spoke of?

"You are in the library of DSA," Erica told the demon.

"DSA?" said the demon. "What's that?"

"Dragon Slayers' Academy," Erica answered.

Wiglaf thought the demon looked confused.

"We are dragon-slayers-in-training," Erica added.

"Oh, right." The demon snorted and gave a strange demonic laugh. "You guys believe in dragons?"

"*Believe* in them?" Erica said. "Pray, sir, how could we not believe in them? We see them almost every day."

"Get out of here," said the demon.

Wiglaf gasped. The demon was telling them to go! Well, he for one was ready.

But Erica stood her ground. "I beg your pardon, sir," she said. "Are you ordering us out of our own library?"

"Sorry. That was just an expression." The demon frowned. "By the way, what year is this again?"

Wiglaf glanced at Angus and Erica. They couldn't help but laugh. Clearly this was only a demon-in-training!

"Do you not even know the year?" asked Erica.

"Of course I know the year," the demon said. "But tell me anyway."

Wiglaf narrowed his eyes. What sort of trick was he up to?

"'Tis but two days before the millennium," Erica told the demon. "The year is 999."

The demon thumped himself in the head with the palm of his hand. The year 999 seemed to surprise him very much. Then he tried to pull himself together.

"My name is Zack," he said. "What's yours?"

"Eric," said Erica. "These are my friends. This is Angus. His uncle is Mordred, our headmaster. And this is Wiglaf. He is our newest student. He has already killed two dragons."

"Whatever," Zack mumbled.

Wiglaf felt proud that Erica had thought to mention his dragons. And he felt that he must now show some bravery—even if he did not feel it. He managed to take a step closer to Zack.

"If you are not a demon," he said, "then, pray, how did you pop out of that book?"

"I don't know," Zack said. "There I was in the library on Forty-second Street, studying for a history test, working on a computer, and—"

"A computer?" said Wiglaf. "Pray, what is a computer?"

"Uh..." Zack thought for a moment. "A computer is kind of a combination of an electric typewriter and a TV."

"Electric?" said Erica.

"Typewriter?" said Angus.

"TV?" said Wiglaf.

All three stared at Zack.

"Okay, I'll explain all that some other time," Zack said. "Anyway, one minute I was using a computer and looking at stuff about your school—the Dragon Slayers' Academy. The next minute, I lose my balance and fall into the computer and wind up here. By the way, where *is* here?"

"Just off Huntsman's Path," Wiglaf answered. "Not far from the Dark Forest. The closest town is Toenail."

"Pray, where do you come from?" Erica asked.

"From New York City," Zack said.

"There is no such place," Angus said.

"No, of course not," Zack said. "Not now, I mean. But there *will* be."

What is he talking about? Wiglaf wondered.

"Look," Zack said, "I came here from a city way in the future. From a city in the year 1999."

"He's lying!" said Angus. "*I* know why he is here!"

Wiglaf and Erica turned and stared at Angus.

"Why is he here?" they both asked at once.

"Do you not remember the prophecy that Yorick read?" Angus pulled out Yorick's parchment. He waved it in front of their faces.

"What prophecy?" asked Zack. "And who's Yorick?"

"'Tis a prophecy about the world ending," Angus said. He waved it in front of Zack.

Zack took the parchment and began reading it aloud.

> "*The year 1000 fast approaches,*
> *None will survive except the roaches.*
> *Say hello to Armageddon,*
> *For that is where we're surely headin'—*
> *Earthquakes, firestorms, flaming pits,*
> *Black plague, brown plague, gas pains, zits.*
> *How to know the world will end?*
> *Beware these signs, my frightened friend:*
> *When chickens bark and dogs me-ow,*
> *When pig-faced calf is born to cow—*"

"Chickens in East Armpittsia have already started barking like dogs," Angus put in.

"And a dog in Pinwick was heard me-owing like a cat," Wiglaf added.

Just then they heard someone yelling down in the castle yard. They raced to the slit in the castle wall to see what was going on.

"It's Yorick the duck again," observed Angus.

"Doom! Doom!" cried Yorick the duck. "A milkmaid in West Wartswallow has heard tell of a cow in North Ninnyshire that gave birth to a pig-faced calf!"

Erica turned to Zack. "You see?" she said. "Another part of the prophecy has come true!"

"And now you pop out of the pages of a book," Angus went on. "Could it be any clearer? Strange things are happening all over the place, because the world is about to end!"

Wiglaf swallowed. Angus was right. Zack had to be part of the prophecy of doom! Oh, woe were they!

"Who wrote that prophecy stuff?" Zack asked. "It sounds phony-baloney to me."

"We know not who wrote it," Wiglaf said. "But all is not lost, for Count Upsohigh has figured out a way to save us."

"What's that?" asked Zack.

Wiglaf leaned toward him and whispered, "The Golden Hippopotamus."

"The Golden *what*?" asked Zack.

"Everyone in the land is to give Count Upsohigh all the gold they can find," Wiglaf explained. "He will make a big gold hippopotamus. At the stroke of midnight, the count shall break the mold. And the Golden Hippopotamus will save us all."

"Listen," Zack said. "That makes absolutely no sense. The world isn't going to end, whether you give this Count Upsohigh all your gold or not."

"How do you know that?" asked Wiglaf.

"Because I'm from the year 1999," Zack said. "If the world had ended in the year 1000, would I be alive now?"

"He is not alive!" shouted Angus. "He is a demon!"

"Oh, stuff a sock in it, Angus," Zack muttered.

"Stuff a sock in what?" asked Angus.

"Never mind," Zack said. Then he added, "Count Upsohigh is a big fake. I was reading about him just before I got here."

The three of them looked at Zack. They were pretty sure this was just another trick.

"Look. I'll prove to you that I'm from the future. Look at my sneakers."

"Your what?" asked Wiglaf.

"My shoes." Zack pointed to his strange black-and-white boots. "Have you ever seen anything like these?"

"Never," said Wiglaf.

Angus shook his head.

"What manner of thing are they?" Erica asked.

"They're Nikes," Zack said.

"Nike's!" cried Angus. "Behold! These shoes once belonged to Nike, Greek goddess of victory! Who but a demon could steal the shoes of a goddess?"

"Angus," said Zack, "you're really starting to bug me."

Wiglaf thought Zack sounded mad at Angus. He did not think it was a good idea to make a demon mad. What was he saying about bugs? Did he intend to send a plague of locusts upon them? Wiglaf caught Angus's eye.

"Do not anger the Zack," he whispered. "There is no telling what he might do if he gets mad."

Meanwhile, Zack reached into the pockets of his leggings. He pulled out a small package wrapped in parchment. He unwrapped the parchment. Inside was a mysterious cube. It was the color of a pink petunia blossom.

"What is that?" Angus asked eagerly. "A sweet?"

"It's bubblegum," Zack answered. "It won't be invented for another nine hundred and fifty years."

Zack popped the cube into his mouth.

Wiglaf, Angus, and Erica watched closely as Zack chewed.

Wiglaf sniffed. The thing had a strange sweet scent.

Suddenly a pink bulge appeared in Zack's mouth. It began to grow rapidly.

Wiglaf, Erica, and Angus backed away.

"A boil!" cried Angus. "The demon has the plague! The prophecy of doom has begun!"

Chapter 4

iglaf ran out of the library. Angus and Erica were right behind him. They zoomed down the winding tower staircase.

"Hey, wait!" the plague-ridden demon called after them. "Come back!"

But the three never stopped for an instant. They reached the bottom of the stairs and kept running.

Wiglaf ran with speed he never knew he had. The three burst out of the castle into the castle yard, where Class II boys were cleaning cobblestones.

Wiglaf glanced over his shoulder. The demon was still after them. Now Wiglaf saw that the boil had burst. The demon's face was covered with hideous pink slime.

The demon cut across the part of the yard that had just been scrubbed. He slipped on the slick cobblestones and fell. Two of the Class II boys stopped scrubbing and helped him up. But when they saw the ooze on the demon's face, they shrank back.

"I don't have boils!" Zack shouted. He tried to rub the pink off his face. "I don't have the plague!"

"Boils!" cried the Class II boys. "The plague!" They began running in all directions.

Wiglaf, Erica, and Angus ran through the gatehouse and across the drawbridge. Wiglaf led the way to Huntsman's Path. He didn't know how long he might run. He didn't care. He only knew he had to escape.

"The demon is gaining on us!" Erica cried.

"What do you expect?" Angus panted. "He is wearing the shoes of a goddess. Hey, slow down! Do not desert me!"

Wiglaf and Erica glanced at each other. They were not the sort to leave a friend in trouble. They slowed down.

The demon kept running. He quickly caught up with them.

"Hey, guys!" Zack called. His cheeks and chin were still coated with the remains of his boil. "I'm glad you stopped. Now I can prove to you that I don't have... that I don't have..."

But Wiglaf, Erica, and Angus were not listening to the demon. They had frozen in their tracks. For something even scarier than a plague-sick demon hovered just ahead of them on Huntsman's Path.

It was a dragon.

The most gigantic dragon Wiglaf had ever seen.

The three dragon-slayers-in-training dove behind the nearest boulder.

Zack dove after them.

The four huddled together as the beast thrashed its long, spiked tail. It spread huge, bat-like wings. Its neck grew ever longer as it lifted its huge head up, up, up to peer over the rock at them.

"G-g-guys," Zack managed. "W-what are we going to do?"

Erica turned toward Zack. "*Now* do you believe in dragons?" she asked.

Wiglaf groaned. This was no time for Erica to get on one of her I-told-you-so jags.

"I believe, I believe," Zack whispered. "But what are we going to do?"

Wiglaf almost felt sorry for Zack. He sounded a lot like a very scared boy. Not like a demon at all.

"Why ask us?" Wiglaf said.

"You're the dragon slayers," Zack pointed out.

"This isn't a dragon we know," Erica told him.

"You need an introduction to slay it?" Zack asked.

"You do not understand," Wiglaf said. "Every dragon in this kingdom has a name. And every dragon has a secret weakness. That is part of what we learn here at DSA—and we do not know who this one is."

"Why not just *ask* its name?" Zack suggested.

Wiglaf was surprised to see Erica nod. She stood up and stepped out from behind the rock. She cupped her hands to her mouth.

"Halloooo there, good sir dragon!" she yelled. "Pray, what is your name?"

Had the demon cast a spell of insanity on Erica? Wiglaf wondered. This was no way to talk to a dragon!

The dragon opened its mouth. It breathed out a burst of fire.

Erica leaped back behind the rock. The four hit the dirt.

Wiglaf heard a nearby tree sizzle. Then— BOOM! It exploded in a shower of sparks. Hot cinders rained down on their heads.

"WHO DARES TO ASK MY NAME?" thundered the beast.

Wiglaf, Erica, and Angus knew better than to answer an angry dragon.

But Zack evidently did not. He raised his head. He spit dirt out of his mouth. He said, "Four really nice polite boys."

Wiglaf hunched up his shoulders. He waited for the dragon to spew a fireball at Zack. He didn't have to wait long. WHOOSH! Their boulder was hit! It grew red with the heat and then—BAM! It burst into a million pieces.

Now their cover was gone. The four scrambled to their feet as rock chips and pebbles showered down on their heads. They stood face-to-face with the dragon. The angry, fire-spitting dragon.

"FOUR REALLY NICE POLITE BOYS?" the dragon boomed. "FOUR REALLY NICE POLITE BOYS WHO WANT TO KNOW MY NAME? WHY? TO INVITE ME TO A FANCY DINNER? TO INVITE ME TO A BALL AT THE CASTLE? NO, TO FIND OUT ABOUT

ME SO YOU CAN KILL ME! FOUR REALLY NICE POLITE BOYS, INDEED!"

The dragon spit out another mouthful of flames. The fire hit the sandy path in front of Zack and the dragon-slayers-in-training. Instantly, the sand melted and hardened into glass. A cloud of steam rose slowly from Huntsman's Path.

To Wiglaf's amazement, Zack started talking again.

"Okay," Zack said to the dragon. "Part of what you said was true. I admit that. The part about killing you was true."

Wiglaf, Erica, and Angus hit the dirt again. They waited for the dragon to obliterate them all.

But nothing happened.

"It was only because we were afraid," Zack went on. "We were afraid because we thought you were going to kill *us*."

Wiglaf peeked out between his fingers. He saw the dragon's face. It looked angrier than ever. He wished that Zack would disappear back into the page of a book. Or into the trunk of a tree. He didn't really care where. So long as he vanished.

"YOU SEE A DRAGON AND RIGHT AWAY YOU THINK IT WANTS TO KILL YOU?" the dragon asked Zack. "WITHOUT EVEN ASKING? YOU KNOW WHAT THAT IS?"

"What?" asked Zack.

"IT'S PREJUDICE!" cried the beast. "PREJUDICE AGAINST DRAGONS!"

Now Erica jumped up. "But, good sir dragon," she said. "All the other dragons we've met *did* want to kill us."

"I AM NOT ALL THE OTHER DRAGONS YOU'VE MET," the dragon answered saucily. "AND PLEASE—DO NOT ADDRESS ME AS 'GOOD SIR DRAGON.' MY NAME IS EDITH."

"Okay, Edith," Zack said. "Speaking for all of us, we are really sorry that we misjudged you.

We had no idea you never kill boys like us."

Wiglaf rolled his eyes. Ten minutes ago, Zack claimed not to believe in dragons. Now he was talking to this one like some long-lost friend.

"DID I SAY THAT?" thundered dragon Edith. "IS THAT WHAT I SAID, THAT I *NEVER* KILL BOYS LIKE YOU? I DID NOT SAY 'NEVER.'"

"So, uh, you *sometimes* kill boys like us?" Zack asked. He looked around. He seemed to be trying to find another rock to hide behind. But Edith had pretty much taken care of any and all rocks, trees, shrubs, and even blades of grass in the area.

"NOT RECENTLY," dragon Edith said. "NOT FOR...LET'S SEE, AT LEAST SIX HUNDRED YEARS NOW. NOT SINCE I GAVE UP EATING MEAT."

"Good," said Zack.

"I'VE ALWAYS HAD A POLICY," the dragon went on. "EAT WHAT YOU KILL. IT'S

LIKE I TELL MY FELLOW DRAGONS: THE SUPPLY OF BOYS WON'T LAST FOREVER. THEY'RE ALREADY ON THE ENDANGERED LIST. WELL, I BETTER GET BACK TO WORK. MY COFFEE BREAK WAS OVER FIVE MINUTES AGO."

Wiglaf thought that Edith was unlike the other dragons he had met. She sounded almost kind. He felt bold enough to ask her a question.

"Pray, Edith," he said. "Why would you need to work? Do not all dragons have a huge pile of gold?"

Before Wiglaf knew what was happening, Edith shot out her left claw and grabbed him around the middle. She whisked him up, off the ground. She gripped him tighter and tighter.

"Stop!" Wiglaf gasped. "I cannot breathe!"

Chapter 5

"Iiiiiiiiiiiiiiiiiiiiiiiiiiiiiiiiiiii!" cried Wiglaf as the dragon raised him higher and higher. She started squeezing harder.

Wiglaf felt dizzy with fear. Edith seemed determined to squeeze the very life out of him!

He felt himself go limp in the dragon's claw. Edith brought Wiglaf close to her face.

"WHY WOULD YOU BE ASKING ME SUCH A QUESTION?" she demanded.

"W-w-why?" Wiglaf managed. "J-j-just making c-c-conversation. That is all."

"IT WOULDN'T BE BECAUSE YOUR HEADMASTER ORDERED YOU TO FIND

LOTS OF GOLD FOR COUNT UPSOHIGH, WOULD IT?" Edith asked. "IT WOULDN'T BE BECAUSE YOU PLANNED TO STEAL GOLD FROM *ME*, WOULD IT?"

"N-n-no!" Wiglaf cried. "I s-s-swear it!" Before he thought better of it, another question popped out of his mouth. "B-but how do you know about our headmaster and Count Upsohigh?"

"I KNOW EVERYTHING, WIGLAF!" Edith shouted. "AND YOU WON'T FIND ANY GOLD IN MY CAVE. I DON'T KEEP CASH AROUND THE HOUSE ANYMORE. IT ISN'T SAFE. NOT WITH CROOKS LIKE COUNT UPSOHIGH ON THE LOOSE. I PUT ALL *MY* GOLD INTO THE STOCK MARKET AGES AGO."

"See? I told you Count Upsohigh was a crook!" Zack cried from below. Then he turned toward the dragon. "The stock market won't be invented for hundreds of years."

"THEN I GUESS I GOT INTO THE

MARKET AT THE RIGHT TIME, HUH?"
Edith replied.

Wiglaf felt her loosen her grip still more. Ah!
It was good to breathe again.

"Headmaster Mordred said we must find all
the gold we can," Erica told the dragon. "He
said we are to take it to Castle Cashalot by
tomorrow at midnight."

"THEN HEADMASTER MORDRED IS A
FOOL," Edith said.

Wiglaf felt her grip loosen even more. And
more. And...

"*Ayiiiiiiiiiiiiiiiiiiiii!*" Wiglaf cried as the dragon
let go of him entirely.

He hit the ground with a thud.

"Ooof!" he yelped as his breath was knocked
out of him.

"*HASTA LA VISTA*, BABIES!" Edith cried.

Wiglaf felt a rush of wind as she flapped her
wings and flew off. He raised his head and
watched her soar into the sky. Then suddenly:
BOOM! The dragon seemed to explode in

midair! A huge canopy of sparks lit the sky in the spot where she had been. And when the sparks flickered out, the sky was empty.

Erica and Angus rushed over to where Wiglaf lay. Zack was right on their heels.

"Are you all right, Wiglaf?" Erica asked, bending over him.

"I—I think so," Wiglaf managed. "I shall let you know in about a week."

Erica stood up. "You were very brave facing that dragon, Zack," she said.

"Thanks," said Zack. "So were you."

Wiglaf groaned. What about him? Was there no one to say that *he* was brave for having survived a close encounter with Edith?

"I suppose you are not a demon after all," Angus told Zack. Wiglaf thought he sounded a bit disappointed.

"No, I'm a boy," Zack said. "Just like you."

Wiglaf heard a bell ringing far away. At least he hoped a bell was ringing. For if it was not, then he had a serious head injury.

"What's that?" Zack asked.

"The dinner bell," Erica said. She gazed at him for a moment. Then she added, "Zack, are you sure you do not have the plague?"

"I'm sure," Zack replied.

"Then come back to the castle with us," Erica said. "I want you to meet Headmaster Mordred. I want you to convince him that you are from the future. And that the world is not going to end tomorrow night."

Wiglaf lay where he was. He watched Erica and Zack walk toward DSA, chatting. He wondered how much it was going to hurt when he tried to get up. On a scale of 1 to 10, he guessed it would be about a 15.

Angus appeared. He held out a hand. Wiglaf grabbed it. Slowly, slowly Angus pulled him to his feet.

"Are you badly hurt?" Angus asked him. "Are your bones broken?"

"I think not," Wiglaf said. "Yet I am very sore."

Together, the two made their way slowly toward Dragon Slayers' Academy.

"I guess Zack is not a demon," Wiglaf said as they reached the drawbridge.

"No," said Angus. "A demon would have put up a much better fight against the dragon."

The two boys made their way to the DSA dining hall. On the way, they passed Mordred's office. They heard voices inside.

"Zack," Erica was saying, "I should like to present our headmaster, Mordred the Marvelous."

Angus cracked open the door to the headmaster's office. He and Wiglaf slipped inside.

"Pray, Zack," Erica said, "tell Sir Mordred where you come from."

"I come from New York," Zack said. "From a city a thousand years in the future. From the year 1999."

Mordred's violet eyes bulged as he stared at Zack. He thoughtfully scratched the hair that grew on the back of his neck.

"How could you be from the future?" Mordred asked. "The prophecy is that the world is going to end at the end of 999."

"But the world isn't going to end then," Zack told Mordred. "I'm going to be taking a history test the first week of the year 2000." Zack frowned. Wiglaf thought he looked worried. Then Zack added, "If I ever make it back to 1999, that is."

"If the world is not going to end at the end of 999," Mordred said, "then, pray, why would Count Upsohigh tell us to give him all our gold?"

"Take a wild guess," said Zack. "Look, I read about this Count Upsohigh. The history books say he was a big crook."

Wiglaf saw that Mordred's face was turning a very dangerous shade of red.

"You are mistaken!" the headmaster cried. "I do not give gold to crooks! To do so would mean that I was stupid." He glared at Zack. "Do you think I am stupid?"

Zack thought for a moment. "Well, maybe not stupid," he said at last. "More like totally clueless."

"What?" Mordred roared. "I will not tolerate such rudeness! Off to the dungeon with you!"

The headmaster grabbed him by the front of his shirt.

"Hey!" Zack yelled. "Let go of me!"

But Mordred held on tight.

Zack tried to pull away.

Then RRRRRIIIIIIP!

Zack's shirt tore down the middle.

"Zounds!" said Wiglaf.

"Yoiks!" said Angus.

"Gadzooks!" said Erica. "Look at his tunic!"

Chapter 6

iglaf, Erica, and Angus stared at Zack. Mordred's violet eyes bulged as he backed away from the boy.

"What?" Zack said. "What are you all looking at?"

"Your undertunic," Erica answered, pointing.

"My what?" said Zack. Then he looked down at the T-shirt he had on under his shirt. And he smiled.

Mordred squinted at Zack's T-shirt. "What in the...?"

"Let me read it for you, Uncle," Angus offered. "It says NEW YORK YANKEES, 1998 WORLD SERIES CHAMPIONS."

"What are Yankees?" Wiglaf asked.

"A major league baseball team," Zack answered.

"Major league?" said Angus.

"Baseball?" said Erica.

"Oh, boy," Zack muttered. Then he drew a breath. "The Yankees are my favorite team in baseball. Baseball is this really exciting sport," he explained.

"Like jousting?" asked Erica.

"Even better," said Zack. "At the end of the year, the best two baseball teams battle each other for the championship. It's called the World Series. It's like a tournament. In 1998, the Yankees won the World Series."

"The fact that his tunic has the year 1998 on it proves Zack was telling the truth," Erica told the headmaster. "He really *is* from the future."

"Hmmmm," said Mordred. He scratched his chin thoughtfully.

Zack tucked his ripped tunic back into the waistband of his blue leggings.

"And that means the world is not going to end tomorrow," Angus added.

"*Hmmmm*," said Mordred.

"And that means," said Wiglaf, "we do not have to give Count Upsohigh any of our gold."

Before anyone knew what was happening, Mordred yanked his sword from its scabbard. He pointed it at Zack.

Zack jumped back.

"What the heck are you doing?" he cried.

Tears sprang to Mordred's violet eyes.

"Zack," the headmaster said in a voice filled with feeling, "you have done a tremendous service for me...I mean, for the whole world." He wiped tears from his cheek with the back of his hand. "I believe you. I believe the count is a crook. And the world is not going to end. You have saved me from giving away my precious gold. That would have been a fate worse than death! And so, I am going to make you an honorary knight."

Mordred tapped Zack's head with his sword. He tapped his right shoulder. Then his left.

"I hereby dub thee Sir Zack, Honorary Knight of the Dragon Slayers' Academy," Mordred said.

"Well, thanks," said Zack.

Wiglaf thought he looked very pleased.

"And now, let us be off to the dining hall for supper," Mordred said. "Tonight we are having a special treat—Rat Tail Soup and Eel Supreme."

"You know," Zack said, "I'd really love to stay, but I should be getting back to 1999. If I don't get back soon, my dad is going to freak out."

Freak out? Wiglaf rather liked these expressions of Zack's.

"And," Zack went on, "I really have to study for that stupid history test. So I was hoping you'd have some ideas about getting me home."

Mordred's face fell. "I see," he said. "Are you *sure* you cannot stay? Just think what fine publicity you would be for my school. A boy from the future." Mordred gave Zack his most appealing smile. "I could give you a break on the tuition."

Zack shook his head. "Sorry," he said. "So how do I get out of here?"

"You take Huntsman's Path south—" Mordred began.

"No," Zack said. "I mean how do I get myself back to 1999?"

"Ah." Mordred said. "I have absolutely no idea. Not a clue."

"Sir?" said Wiglaf. "Why not summon Zelnoc the wizard?" He turned to Zack. "If anybody can get you to the future, it is a wizard."

"How do I summon this Zelnoc guy?" Zack asked.

"Simple," said Wiglaf. "The way you summon any wizard. You say his name backwards three times. Backwards, Zelnoc is Conlez."

"Conlez...Conlez...Conlez," Zack said quickly.

At the sound of the third "Conlez," a light flashed. It was followed by a puff of white smoke. The smoke turned blue. It whirled itself into a tornado, and Zelnoc lurched out of the spinning smoke. Wiglaf thought he looked quite dizzy. As always, the wizard wore a blue robe dotted with silver stars. His pointed hat sat crookedly on his head of white hair.

"Suffering succotash!" Zelnoc cried. "Why must I always be summoned smack-dab in the middle of dinner?" He patted his lips with a napkin he still held in his hand. He frowned at Zack. Then he turned his gaze upon Wiglaf.

"Oh, it is *you* again, Piglaugh," he said.

"It's *Wig*laf," Zack corrected him.

"Whatever," said Zelnoc. "What is it you wish this time, Wiglap?"

"WigLAF," said Zack.

Then Wiglaf piped in. "Our friend Zack wishes to return to the future. Can you do that sort of thing?"

"Can I *do* that sort of thing?" Zelnoc scoffed. "Of *course* I can do that sort of thing. What year do you wish to travel to, Riffraff?"

"His name is *Wiglaf*," Zack said. "And he's not the one who wants to go to the future, Zelnoc. It's me. I'm Zack."

Zelnoc looked annoyed. "Well, make up my mind," he said. "I have to get back to my dinner. Now, what year do you wish to travel to, Zeke?"

"It's *Zack*," said Zack. "And I want to get back to the year 1999."

"Peachy," said Zelnoc. "All right, get all your tearful goodbyes out of the way, and I shall send you right back there, Jack."

"*Zack*," said Zack. He looked around the office. "Well, goodbye, everybody," he said. "It's been great. Here's something to remember me by." Zack reached into his pocket. He pulled out three pieces of bubblegum. He gave one to Wiglaf, one to Erica, and one to Angus. "It's a little present from the future. And since I won't be around...Happy New Year!" He turned toward the wizard. "Okay, Zelnoc," he added. "I'm out of here."

"Curious," said Zelnoc, blinking. "I could swear I still see you."

"That's just an expression," said Zack. "It means I'm ready to go. Now how do we do this?"

"I have the directions right here," said Zelnoc. He stuffed his napkin up his sleeve. Then he reached deep into the pocket of his robe. He took out a scrap of parchment. He began to read aloud. "'One hundred percent cotton, hand wash separately in cold water, dark colors may run.' No, that's not it. Wait a minute."

The wizard reached into his pocket a second time. He pulled out another small piece of parchment. Once more he began to read: "'In a two-quart saucepan, combine three cups water, two tablespoons butter, one package Spicy Rice Pilaf, and bring to a boil...' Drat! That's not it either." Zelnoc looked sheepishly at Zack. "Sorry."

Zack just shrugged. But Wiglaf thought he looked worried.

Zelnoc reached into his pocket a third time. He brought out yet another scrap of parchment. This time he read it to himself before he began to read aloud.

"Ah, yes, here we are," he said. "Pray, pay attention now, Zook."

"*Zack*," said Zack. "And believe me, I'm paying attention."

And Zelnoc began to read:

"*If to another time you'd go,*
Heed directions found below:
Close your eyes and hold your breath
Till you're somewhat close to death.
When your skin's a lovely blue,
This is what you needs must do:
Rub your tummy, pat your gizzard,
Bow politely to your wizard,
Spin around and don't be cautious,
Go so fast it makes you nauseous.
Scream and yell and wail and screech.
Then shout the year you wish to reach."

Zelnoc glanced up from the parchment. "Did you remember all of that?" he asked Zack.

Zack nodded. "I guess so," he said.

"Then go ahead and do it," the wizard instructed.

Zack closed his eyes. He held his breath. He did it for a long time. Wiglaf thought he was starting to look a bit blue. Then Zack began rubbing his stomach. He patted his neck. Clearly he thought that was his gizzard. He bowed to Zelnoc and started spinning. He spun slowly at first and then started going faster and faster. He stumbled unsteadily and shouted out, "1999!"

Wiglaf held his own breath as he stared at Zack. One minute he was spinning and lurching around the DSA headmaster's office. And the next minute—POOF! The boy from the future vanished into thin air.

Chapter 7

"oys!" Mordred boomed. "'Tis the last day of 999! Get up! Get out of bed!"

Wiglaf sat halfway up in his cot. It was still dark outside. What was the headmaster doing in the Class I dorm, rousting them out of bed before dawn?

"On the double!" Mordred kept on. "It'll take us all day to march to Toenail. We must start right away!"

"But, Uncle!" Angus cried. "Remember what Zack said? You need not take your gold to Count Upsohigh."

"True," Mordred replied. He sat down heavily on his nephew's cot. "*Oof!*" he cried. "This bed is as lumpy as one of Frypot's puddings! It's a good thing boys don't mind where they sleep." He eyed Angus. "Think on this, nephew. Everyone from hither and yon will be bringing gold to Toenail. There will be wagons and oxcarts and wheelbarrows chock full of it!" Mordred sighed happily. A dazed look crept over his face.

Angus waved a hand in front of Mordred's staring violet eyes. "Uncle?" he said. "Are you all right?"

"What?" Mordred snapped out of his trance. "Where was I? Oh, yes. I'm counting on you and your friends."

"To do what, sir?" asked Erica.

"To spread the word that Mordred the Marvelous says no one need give any gold to Count Upsohigh," the headmaster said.

"All right, Uncle," said Angus.

"And then," Mordred went on, "tell folks that there is a way they can show me how thankful they are."

"And how can they, sir?" asked Wiglaf .

"They can give their gold to *me*!" Mordred boomed.

"But, sir—" Wiglaf began.

"*Shhh!*" Mordred held a finger to his lips. "Tell them they can keep a teensy-weensie bit of their gold. It's more than they would have had if they'd given it all to Upsohigh. Am I right?"

Wiglaf, Angus, and Erica nodded.

"So get the message out. Or..." Mordred's smile changed to a frown. "...woe upon your heads! I'll settle for nothing less that a whopping wheelbarrow piled high with gold!"

Mordred the Marvelous popped up. "Well, what are you waiting for, boys? Let's *move!*"

The Class I boys quickly dressed. They grabbed their swords. Wiglaf, Angus, and Erica ran with the others down the stairs to the dining hall. But no breakfast awaited them. Instead, Frypot had packed little bags of eel-on-a-bun-to-go.

"A good breakfast is the key to a good day!"

Frypot said. He handed them their unhappy meals. "*Bon appetit!*"

Minutes later, everyone marched out of the DSA castle yard and down the drawbridge. They headed north on Huntsman's Path.

Wiglaf worried as he marched. Maybe they could convince people not to give Count Upsohigh their gold. But could they talk them into giving their gold to Mordred? Impossible!

Huntsman's Path grew crowded. All sorts of folks were on their way to Toenail: cabbage farmers and blacksmiths, shoemakers and milkmaids, cheese mongers and pastry bakers, friars and hangmen. Every one of them carried a pouch or a box or a purse full of gold. One and all seemed willing to give Count Upsohigh their gold to keep the world from ending.

Just before sunset, Wiglaf spied the famous Toenail landmark: Big Toe Tower. It was the world's tallest building—a full three stories high! And at its top stood a huge hourglass.

"I see gold! Beautiful, beautiful gold!"

Mordred pressed his fist to his mouth to keep himself from yelping with joy. "Get that gold for me, boys! Get it! Meet me with it at Big Toe just after midnight!" That said, the headmaster broke into a run, leaving his boys behind in his dust.

Soon the DSA students entered the gates of Toenail. Hundreds of torches lit the path to the town square. They made their way toward the center of town.

"So many people!" Angus exclaimed.

Wiglaf had never been in such a crowd. It was just as Mordred had said it would be. People hurried by with carts and wheelbarrows piled high with gold coins and golden jewelry.

At last the three friends reached the south side of the town square. Wiglaf saw Big Toe at the north end. It towered over everything.

Right in front of them sat a huge black cauldron. A roaring fire crackled under it. The gold knight stood beside the cauldron. People were lined up to give him their gold. He took it and tossed it into buckets. The buckets filled quickly.

"Look, Wiggie," said Erica. "That's Castle Cashalot."

Wiglaf spied the castle on the west side of the square. Its sparkly gold stone shone in the moonlight. The torches inside glowed through its many round windows, making them shine like bright gold coins.

"And look!" cried Angus. "There is the mold for the Golden Hippopotamus!" He pointed toward the middle of the square where it stood. Wiglaf guessed that the beast was as wide as seven horses and as tall as three tall men. Or five short ones.

"We have little time to get Mordred his gold," Angus said. "We must begin our task."

The three hurried over to the long line of people waiting to give the gold knight their gold.

"Mordred the Marvelous says the world is not going to end," Wiglaf told a waiting milkmaid. "You can keep your gold."

"Mordred the who?" The milkmaid rolled her eyes and handed her small purse to the knight.

Wiglaf tried again. "Stop!" he told a shepherd. "You need not give the count your gold. The world is not going to end!"

"What about the pig-faced calf?" the shepherd asked.

"Did you see it yourself?" asked Wiglaf.

"Not me," said the shepherd. "But the son of my second cousin is engaged to a girl who once passed through the town next to the village where the unfortunate calf was born."

"Yes, but—" Wiglaf got no further. The shepherd tossed his two golden coins into the gold knight's bucket.

Angus and Erica ran up to Wiglaf.

"No one will listen to me," Erica said.

"Me, either," said Wiglaf.

"What can we do?" Angus moaned. "Uncle Mordred will be most unhappy."

"Zounds! Look!" Erica exclaimed. "'Tis the

Kingdom Criers, Lady Katherine and Sir Matthew."

Wiglaf saw that indeed a stage had been set up at the north side of the town square, right under Big Toe. Lady Katherine and Sir Matthew sat upon the stage on fancy high-backed thrones. They were dressed in silks and velvets.

"Egad!" said Angus. "I have seen the likenesses of Lady Katherine and Sir Matthew on many a message tree. But I never thought to gaze upon their faces so up close and personal."

The three pressed through the crowd to get a better look at the famous criers. And to hear what news they had to tell.

Lady Katherine stood. A hush fell on the crowd.

"Good day, good people!" Lady Katherine said. "Well, Sir Matthew," she added, gazing at the man next to her. "Here it is. The night we've all been waiting for—the Countdown to the Year 1000. Millennium Eve. And what an exciting night it is."

"Gadzooks, right you are, Lady Katherine," Sir Matthew said, getting to his feet. "Never have I seen Toenail look so splendid. Take a gander at that hourglass. Have you ever seen a timepiece of such a size?"

"Never," said Lady Katherine. She looked out at the crowd that was quickly gathering in Toenail Square. "We're going to tell you more about that hourglass—who thought of it, the glassblowers who turned blue from working on it, and many other fascinating details. But right now, we're going to take a little break." The kingdom criers sat down on their thrones.

A small, wiry man rushed out onto the stage. He began scratching his head. He scratched more and more wildly. Then two damsels walked onto the stage. One had long blond hair. The other had brown tresses. They peered at the scratching man.

"Alas, poor Yorick," said the yellow-haired damsel.

Wiglaf squinted. Zounds! The man *was*

Yorick. Wiglaf knew that Mordred paid his scout very little. But he never guessed that Yorick had to take a side job to earn a few extra pennies.

On stage, Yorick scratched his head harder than ever.

"'Tis a pity he hath not heard of Dr. Varmint's Dander-Off," said the brown-haired damsel.

"'Tis a shame," agreed the blond maiden. "Else he would not be a-scratching so."

Both damsels now brought big flasks out from the wide sleeves of their gowns.

"Try Dr. Varmint's Dander-Off," they said together. "And your itch will be gone!"

Yorick lifted off what Wiglaf hoped was a wig and shouted, "And so will your hair!"

Then all three ran off the stage.

Sir Matthew and Lady Katherine stood up again.

"We are back with the Countdown to the Year 1000," Lady Katherine said. "And right now we have a special guest."

"And here he is," Sir Matthew said. "The nobleman who figured out how to save the world, Count Upsohigh!"

Everyone clapped and cheered.

Wiglaf watched as a short, chubby man dressed in gold velvet shuffled out onto the stage.

"Good to have you here, Count Upsohigh," Lady Katherine said. "Tell me, sir. What is happening with the Golden Hippopotamus?"

"My men have been pouring molten gold into the hippo for six days," the count said. "But keep that gold coming, folks. We don't have enough yet. And if that hippo mold isn't filled to the brim with gold, you know what will happen."

"The world will end!" wailed several in the crowd.

"Bingo." The count nodded. "Don't let it happen, folks. Act now. My gold knight is standing by, waiting to take your gold."

"Tell us, Count," said Sir Matthew. "Exactly what will happen at the stroke of midnight?"

"Twelve men with big hammers will be waiting beside the hippopotamus mold," Count Upsohigh said. "At the last bell of midnight, they will swing their hammers and break the mold. One and all shall feast their eyes upon the Golden Hippopotamus! And the world shall be saved!"

Wiglaf glanced at the hourglass. Even less sand was left in it now. Soon, Count Upsohigh would have everyone's gold. And when midnight came and the world did not end, everyone would be grateful to the count for saving them. Thinking of it made Wiglaf so mad.

"We must do something to stop Count Upsohigh," Wiglaf whispered to his friends.

"You're right," agreed Angus. "But what?"

Chapter 8

ount Upsohigh talked on and on to the Kingdom Criers.

Wiglaf, Erica, and Angus knew there was no point in listening, so they wandered back toward the cauldron. They watched the gold knight tossing people's gold into buckets. They watched Count Upsohigh's gold-coated servants carry the gold-filled buckets off in the direction of Castle Cashalot. They saw other gold-coated servants carry buckets from the castle over to the cauldron and pour in the gold. Wiglaf idly wondered why there was so much back-and-forth with the buckets.

Wiglaf turned to watch other servants ladle

steaming golden liquid from the cauldron into other buckets. They ran the buckets over to servants standing on ladders that leaned against the sides of the hippopotamus. Those servants poured the liquid gold into the giant mold.

Angus sniffed. "What is that smell?" he asked.

"Boiling gold?" Wiglaf suggested.

Angus shook his head. "I think not." He sniffed again. "'Tis a scent I know from long ago."

"Something odd is going on here," said Erica. "Why is it that the people do not toss their gold directly into the cauldron?"

The three watched the operation in silence.

Wiglaf frowned. "Do you think they could be switching buckets?" he asked, pointing. "Those servants are taking the buckets to Castle Cashalot. Perhaps they are emptying them and filling them with something else. Something that only looks like gold."

The three stared at each other as the meaning of what Wiglaf had said sank in.

"Let us meander over to Castle Cashalot ourselves," Erica suggested. "Perhaps we can figure out what the count is up to."

They made their way closer to the castle. From a distance, they watched Upsohigh's servants carry bucket after bucket of gold into a side entrance of the castle.

The three snuck as close as they dared. But guards were marching up and down in front of the castle. They dared not go too close.

"Stay here," Erica said. She ran off. Before long, she came back. "There is only one guard on patrol at the back of the castle. Come on!"

The three circled around until they were behind the castle. They waited, as a guard marched slowly by. When he was gone, Erica pointed to a window. "If we move quickly, we can look in before the guard gets back. I shall stand on your shoulders, Angus. Wiglaf, you shall stand on my shoulders. Then you can..."

"Fall off and die," Wiglaf muttered.

"No, you shall peek through the window and see what is going on," Erica said.

The guard rounded the corner again. The three hunkered down. The guard passed by without seeing them.

Wiglaf sighed. "All right. Let's get this over with."

They hurried over to the window.

"*Ow*!" Wiglaf cried as he ran into something hard and stubbed his toe. He looked down and frowned. Several large sacks were piled up under the window.

"What's this?" Erica asked as she, too, spied the sacks.

Angus tried to lift one of them.

"*Oof*!" he cried. "This thing weighs a ton!"

Angus managed to untie a rope around one sack. The three peered inside.

"Gold!" they exclaimed.

"Zack was right!" Wiglaf said. "Upsohigh is a crook!"

"Wiggie, look out!" Erica said suddenly.

Wiglaf jumped back as another sack of gold dropped from the window.

THUD!

"Let us be gone!" Wiglaf said. "We must tell Mordred."

"Wait," said Angus. "What's this?" He pulled something out from behind one of the sacks of gold. It was a large traveling trunk. It was marked with the initials C.U.

"Why would Count Upsohigh need a trunk?" asked Wiglaf. "Unless..."

"Unless he is planning to make a quick getaway," Erica finished for him.

"And what's this?" said Angus. He picked up a piece of parchment that lay on top of the trunk. "A ticket!"

Erica plucked it out of his hand. She read out loud: "First-class passage for one on the luxury liner *The Goldfish*." She glanced up at her friends. "The ship sails for Zanzibar at dawn!"

"And Count Upsohigh plans to be on it," Wiglaf exclaimed.

"We shall stop him!" Erica cried. She waved the ticket over her head. "For now we have proof that Upsohigh's Golden Hippopotamus scheme is nothing but a scam!"

Erica grabbed a gold coin from the sack as more proof. Then the three took off for the town square just as the guard turned the corner. They ran past the cauldron. Angus stopped suddenly. He sniffed again. "I know that scent!" he said. "Why can I not place it?"

"Come on," said Erica. She grabbed Angus by the elbow. "We have no time for smells now."

The three pushed and shoved their way through the packed crowd. At last they made it to a spot from which they could see the stage. Count Upsohigh was still on it. He was demonstrating how high he could count.

"Three hundred ninety-nine," Count Upsohigh said proudly. "Four hundred!"

Everyone gasped and looked around.

"Now *that*," said a candle maker standing next to Wiglaf, "is counting."

Wiglaf glanced at the hourglass on Big Toe. Only a small pile of sand was left in the top.

"We have not much time!" he whispered.

"We shall never find Uncle Mordred in this crowd," Angus wailed.

"Forget about Mordred," said Erica. "We must get the ticket and coin to the Kingdom Criers. They can stop Upsohigh!"

"But we can hardly move in this crowd," said Angus. "And besides, no one is allowed anywhere near the Criers."

Wiglaf's heart sank. Angus was right. There were too many people between them and the Criers. And guards stood everywhere around the stage. Now what? He wondered if he had thought to bring along his lucky rag. He put a hand into his pocket. He did not find his rag. But his fingers closed around a small cube wrapped in parchment. Wiglaf smiled.

Moments later, the three had unwrapped the bubblegum that Zack had given them. They popped it into their mouths and began to chew. Wiglaf had no idea how Zack had made this gum into a bubble. He saw that Erica and Angus were puzzled, too. Wiglaf stuck out his tongue. He crossed his eyes and saw that it was covered with a thin pink skin. He blew air under the bubblegum skin and...blew a bubble.

"Wiggie!" Erica exclaimed. "You did it!"

Quickly, Erica blew a bubble of her own.

"Plague victims, coming through!" Angus cried.

The way quickly parted for Wiglaf and Erica.

"Sick folk with hideous boils," Angus cried. "Don't get too close. Very contagious."

"Plague!" People started screaming.

And in no time the three stood right below the stage.

Angus elbowed a guard.

"Plague victims," he said.

The guard dove under the stage.

Erica spat out her gum. She dashed up onto the stage. Count Upsohigh was still counting. Lady Katherine and Sir Matthew looked startled to see Erica approach them. But she gave a small bow and thrust the *S.S. Goldfish* ticket and the coin into Lady Katherine's hand. Erica spoke eagerly to Lady Katherine for some time. Then she dashed away.

Lady Katherine leaned over and whispered something to Sir Matthew. Then she beckoned a guard up onto the stage. She whispered something to him, and he hurried off. Lady Katherine and Sir Matthew stood up.

"Excuse me, Count?" Lady Katherine said.

"Four hundred twenty—huh?" said the count.

"Sorry to interrupt you, sir," Lady Katherine said. "We have late-breaking news."

"What?" Count Upsohigh said as a page escorted him to a chair that had been set up between Lady Katherine and Sir Matthew. "I wasn't even up to five hundred yet. I can count to five hundred, you know."

"So I've heard," said Lady Katherine. "But I wonder if you can answer a few questions for me?"

"Questions?" said Count Upsohigh. "Of course I can answer questions. I am very good at questions."

"Fine," said Sir Matthew. "How did you come up with this Golden Hippopotamus plan?"

"It came to me in a dream," the count said.

Erica pushed her way back to Wiglaf and Angus in the crowd. She gave them a fast thumbs-up.

"Can you explain exactly how this hippopotamus from your dream is going to save the world?" Lady Katherine asked.

"Of course!" boomed the count. "As I said, my men will shatter the mold at midnight. And there will stand the biggest, fattest, heaviest, solidest, goldest hippopotamus the world has ever seen!"

"But, sir," said Lady Katherine, "exactly how does it work?"

Wiglaf smiled to see the count grow flustered.

"Well, er...it is not the sort of thing one can explain," the count said. "But it will work. Oh, yes. It shall save the world from a terrible end!"

"*Hmmmm*," said Lady Katherine. "Well, perhaps you can tell me about this, sir." She held up the ticket. "First-class passage for one on *The Goldfish*. It sails at dawn!"

"How should I know about that ticket?" the count cried. "It certainly is not mine!"

"Oh, really?" said Sir Matthew. "Then why is your trunk all packed?" He nodded in the direction of two Kingdom Crier guards who were carrying Count Upsohigh's trunk up onto the stage.

Wiglaf saw the count tremble at seeing his trunk.

"Perhaps...someone has planned a New Year's surprise for me," the count said. He wiped the sweat from his forehead. "And after I save the world, what's wrong with my taking a little medieval pleasure cruise?"

"That's right!" called someone in the crowd.

"We owe the count our lives!" yelled another. "Three cheers for Upsohigh!"

To Wiglaf's horror, the crowd began to cheer.

"One!" counted the count after the first cheer.

"Two!" he cried after the second.

"Three!" he yelled after the third.

"Count Upsohigh," said Lady Katherine when the cheering died down. "What would you say, sir, if I told you that two dozen bags of gold have been found behind Castle Cashalot?"

"Why...I would...say that I hope whoever owns the gold will bring it to my knight! Get my men to melt it down and add it to the hippopotamus," the count said. "For if it does not have exactly one hundred druckets of gold, the world shall surely end."

"Then the gold does not belong to you?" said Sir Matthew.

"To me?" said the count. "Of course not. I have given every last gluck-glucket of my gold for the Golden Hippopotamus."

"Oh, really?" said Lady Katherine. "Then tell me, sir, how is it that the bags that hold the gold are marked with the initials C.U.?"

She nodded in the direction of a line of guards. Each one carried a bag of gold over his shoulder. The guards marched up onto the stage. They put the monogrammed bags of gold down in front of Count Upsohigh.

"He is sweating now," Angus whispered.

Wiglaf nodded. The count looked very uncomfortable.

"Explain this, sir," said Lady Katherine. She untied the rope from one of the bags. She reached in and pulled out a handful of gold coins and gold jewelry.

The crowd gasped.

"I—I—" the count began. "I can only say—"

BONG!

It was midnight!

The bell in Big Toe Tower had begun to ring:
BONG! BONG! BONG!

Everyone looked away from the count as the twelve hammer men stepped up to the hippo mold.

BONG! BONG! BONG! BONG!

The hammer men drew back their hammers.

BONG! BONG! BONG! BONG!

"It is the year 1000!" Lady Katherine announced. "Happy New Year, everyone!"

"Happy New Millennium!" said Sir Matthew. "The world is alive and well!"

The hammer men slammed their hammers into the hippo mold.

BAM!

The clay cracked and fell to the ground.

And there, glowing in the torchlight, stood the Golden Hippopotamus.

"You see?" cried Count Upsohigh. "The world is beginning a new millennium! And all thanks to me—and to this solid-gold hippopotamus!"

"Not gold!" Angus cried suddenly.

He yelled so loudly that everyone in Toenail turned to stare at him.

"That scent!" Angus cried. "I know it now!" He closed his eyes and took in a long breath. "My mother used to put it on my toast."

Wiglaf shot Erica a look. He feared that all the excitement had been too much for Angus.

Angus sniffed again. "'Tis a pity that Uncle Mordred is too cheap to let us have a little bit of butter."

"Butter?" Erica exclaimed. "Angus, do you mean to say that Count Upsohigh has..."

"Yes," said Angus. "The count has made a hippopotamus of solid butter!"

"Butter?" people in the crowd began to mutter. "Butter?"

They pressed close to the giant beast.

A milkmaid was brave enough to poke the hippo. She licked her finger and nodded. "It's butter, all right," she cried.

"Where is our gold? We want our gold!" the

people howled. Some ran for the bags of gold on the stage. Others headed toward Castle Cashalot where they hoped to find more gold.

Wiglaf saw Count Upsohigh snatch up one bag of gold. Then he jumped off the stage and ran toward the Dark Forest. Wiglaf thought it would be quite some time before he dared to show his face in Toenail again.

Wiglaf, Angus, and Erica watched as everyone dove for the gold. Then came the shoving and pushing and grabbing. The three friends walked through the crowd, slowly making their way to Big Toe. And there on the steps sat Mordred.

The headmaster's velvet tunic was ripped. He had dirt on his face. His hair stuck up at odd angles. He looked battle-worn but, Wiglaf thought, very, very happy.

"I managed to grab a whole wheelbarrow of gold," Mordred explained.

Wiglaf saw that, indeed, Mordred was resting one elbow on a wheelbarrow. But the

wheelbarrow was empty. Wiglaf saw several peasants, the milkmaid, and the shepherd creeping away. They each carried a large, bulging sack.

Uh-oh, thought Wiglaf. He began backing away from Big Toe Tower. He knew better than to say anything. Mordred would find out that the barrow was empty soon enough. Then there would be yelling and shouting and many, many tears. But right now Wiglaf wanted to enjoy the first moments of the new millennium.

People were dancing in Toenail Square. A juggler was tossing eight daggers in the air at once. A minstrel was singing. A pair of fire-eaters were gulping down huge balls of flame.

"Don't freak out, sir," Wiglaf said to Mordred. "But we're out of here." He grabbed Erica and Angus and pulled them toward the town square.

"*Hasta la vista*, babies!" shouted Angus as they ran to celebrate the beginning of the next thousand years. "Happy New Millennium!"